The Albino Bunny Activity Booklet

Hillary A. Hinds

The Albino Bunny Activity Booklet
Written by Hillary A. Hinds

Copyright© 2020 by Hillary A. Hinds

All Scripture quotations are taken from the Holy Bible, King James Version, which is in the public domain.

ISBN:978-1-7771012-6-8

Written by Hillary A. Hinds, Books4dNations Learning Innovations.

Cover Design and Illustrations by StallionSudio88

Puzzles by Hillary A Hinds

Publisher: Books4dNations Learning Innovations

To the Nations' Kids

Love

Hillary

About

The Albino Bunny Activity
Booklet

CLUCK
CLUCK

Match the Picture on the left with the correct word on the right

Bunny

Hen

Frog

Cow

Turtle

Help the Frog to find the Lily pad

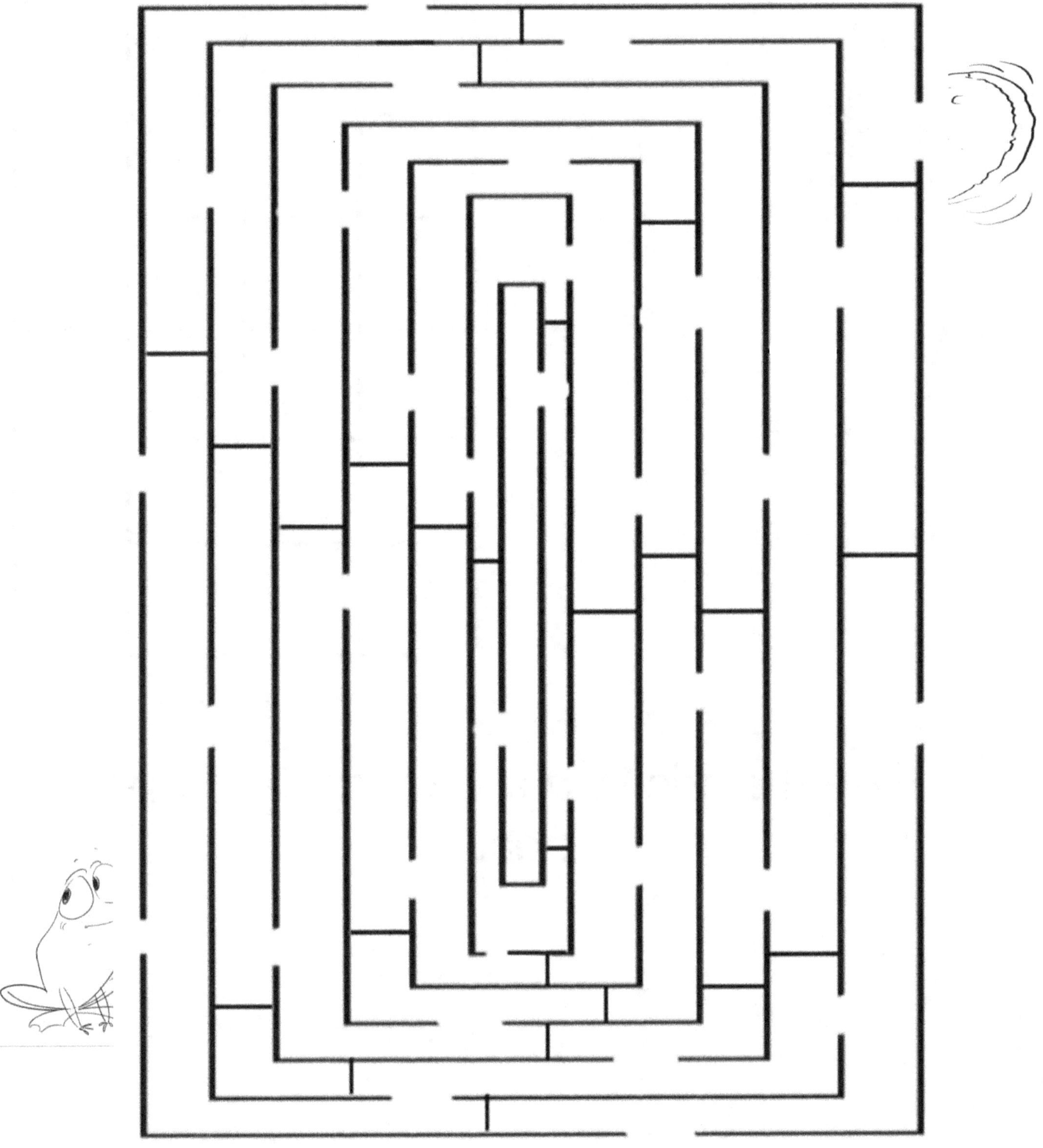

Use the grid to draw a picture of the hen.

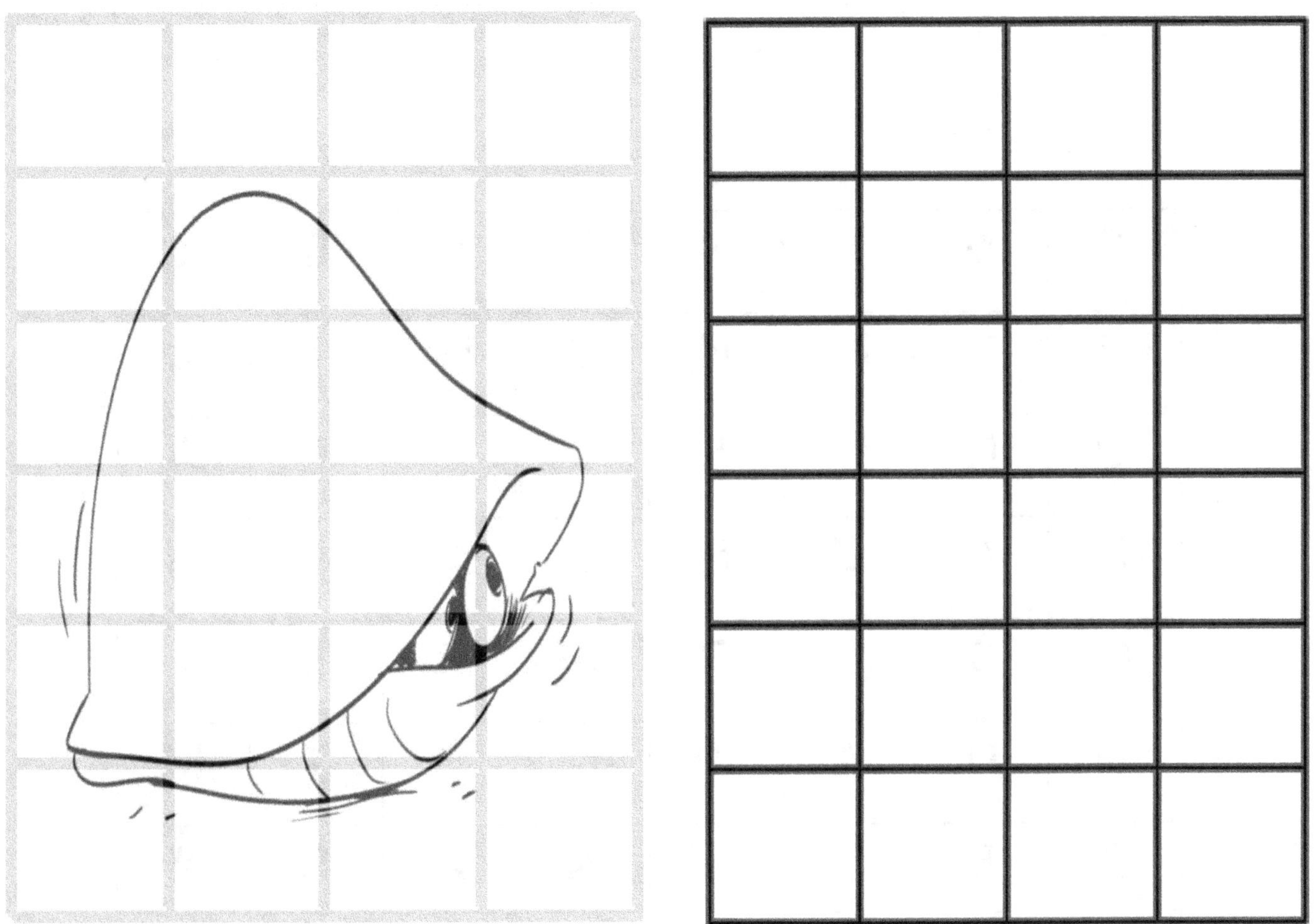

Use the grid to draw a picture of the turtle.

Can you find the hidden words in the puzzle?

E	N	Y	N	N	U	B	S
P	T	M	N	B	W	I	L
O	N	I	E	R	F	R	A
H	C	U	H	O	C	E	N
G	S	O	R	W	R	L	I
O	D	A	W	N	O	T	M
R	E	N	L	A	A	R	A
F	H	N	O	P	K	U	E
Y	L	I	L	P	S	T	L

FROG	BROWN	COW	HEN
SPLASH	ANIMALS	TURTLE	POND
BUNNY	LILY	CROAK	RUN
WHITE	HOP		

Can you find the turtle that is different?

See which animal will get to the pond first.

Unscrambled the Words

1. GOFR   ______________________________

2. ELURT   ______________________________

3. NDPO   ______________________________

4. NBNUY   ______________________________

5. EHN   ______________________________

6. IYLL APD   ____________ -- ___________

7. LEDFSI   ______________________________

8. LCUCK   ______________________________

9. AHSPSL   ______________________________

10. RWBON   ______________________________

Drawing Page

Drawing Page

Drawing Page

Drawing Page

Drawing Page

Drawing Page

Drawing Page

Drawing Page

Drawing Page

____

Drawing Page

"He Has made everything beautiful

in its time."

Ecclesiastes 3: 11 KJV

About the Author

Hillary A Hinds is the author of several children's books, including *Rabbit Goes to Church*. She has also written *It's My Time* inspirational journal and *KidzStrive the Children's Ministry Workbook for Teachers, Parents, and Children*. She was born in Jamaica and currently resides in Canada.

Hillary is the founder of Books4NAtionsKids of Saskatchewan, which provides faith-based books to kids and different charities worldwide.